KUNG FU PANDA
LEGENDS OF AWESOMENESS

nickelodeon

Po's Awesomely Perfect Present

adapted by Tina Gallo

Simon Spotlight
New York London Toronto Sydney New Delhi

SIMON SPOTLIGHT
An imprint of Simon & Schuster Children's Publishing Division
1230 Avenue of the Americas, New York, New York 10020
This Simon Spotlight edition September 2015

For information about special discounts for bulk purchases, please contact Simon & Schuster Special Sales
at 1-866-506-1949 or business@simonandschuster.com.
Manufactured in the United States of America 0815 LAK
2 4 6 8 10 9 7 5 3 1
ISBN 978-1-4814-1732-7 ISBN 978-1-4814-1733-4 (eBook)

It was a busy day in Ping's Noodle Shop. The Furious Five were helping Po's dad prepare for the Winter Festival. There were going to be many guests, so there was a lot of work that needed to be done.

"Po!" Tigress called. "Your father needs you."

"Just a minute . . . almost done . . . ," Po replied. Po was busy making his father a gift.

Po proudly showed Tigress his gift.
"A boomerang?" Tigress guessed.
"No, it's a spoon!" Po said.
Tigress looked confused. "That's a *spoon*?"
Now Po was embarrassed. "I couldn't find a straight piece of wood," he stammered. "And . . ."

Just at that moment Po's dad, Mr. Ping, yelled that he needed Po to bring him some sesame seeds. When Po went looking for the seeds, he found the gift his father had bought for him. It was the nunchakus Po had been wanting forever. Po felt a little guilty. "Dad deserves more than my lousy homemade spoon," he said to himself. "I've got to get him something better."

Mr. Ping handed some small packages to Tigress and Xiao Niao, one of the Winter Festival guests. "I need you to wrap some little presents I got for everyone," he told them.

Xiao Niao smiled at Tigress. "Yay, I love helping!" she said. "Don't you love wrapping presents? It's so creative!" She jumped up and gave Tigress a hug.

Tigress glared at her. "We are *not* going to get along," she said.

Just then Po walked into the room.

"Sweet necklace," he told Xiao Niao.

Xiao Niao giggled. "I know, right?" she said.

Po was looking for Viper. He hurried to her side.

"Viper, you have to help me get my dad a present," he whispered. "All I did was carve him a lousy spoon."

Po showed her the spoon.

"Ohhh. Wow. Yeah, let's hit the marketplace," Viper said.

At the marketplace, Po found the exact gift he wanted to buy his dad. It was a shiny, golden wok.

"It's the most beautiful wok-shaped thing I've ever seen!" Po exclaimed. He turned to the vendor. "How much is it?"

"Five hundred yuan," the vendor said.

"Five hundred!" Po cried. "Where am I going to get—"

"Five hundred yuan!" a voice called out. It was Constable Hu. He was holding up a "Wanted" poster. "I'm offering a five-hundred-yuan reward for the capture of this escaped prisoner!"

Viper looked at the poster and gasped. "It's Shengqi! He's a kung fu master from Muchang Township. Shengqi is definitely not someone you want to mess with, Po."

"But my dad deserves an awesome present," Po said. He turned to Constable Hu. "I'll do it!"

500

Po arrived in Muchang Township and was immediately greeted warmly by the villagers. "Are you here for the Winter Festival feast?" they asked. "We hardly ever get strangers in town for the Winter Festival."

"Great to meet you all!" Po said with a smile. "Actually I'm here looking for Shengqi."

In a flash, all the smiles were gone.

"Hey, where did all the happy faces go?" Po asked. "Now you're all frowny and your eyebrows are all smooshed down."

All the villagers started shouting at Po at once: "Leave Shengqi alone!" "He didn't do anything!" "He's a good guy!"

"I'm sure you guys are only trying to protect a friend, so I have to warn you . . . I'm the Dragon Warrior," Po said.

"You won't get any information out of us," one of the villagers said, "and I am *not* pointing out Shengqi's hut over there."

Po smiled. "Thanks," he said.

Shengqi was hiding from Po, but Po soon spotted him. After fighting for a while, it looked like Po had his prisoner.

Shengqi begged Po, "Please don't turn me in. I must keep my promise to my daughter. Let me explain."

Shengqi said that he was once the bodyguard of Duke Pingjun. At last year's Winter Festival, the duke held a feast for his wealthy friends. An enormous mooncake was served. But one of the serving girls slipped and fell headfirst into the cake, and it was ruined. Furious, the duke went to slap the girl. Shengqi grabbed the duke's hand.

"That girl was my daughter," Shengqi said. And when Shengqi grabbed the duke, the duke stumbled and fell into the cake, and all the guests laughed.

"Because he was embarrassed before his guests, he accused me of assault and had me locked away in prison for life. And that was the last time I saw my daughter," Shengqi said to Po. "I promised her I'd get back to her for the next Winter Festival."

"That's a sad story," Po said. "Almost as sad as my present for my dad."

"Po, it's not how nice the present is that matters," Shengqi said, "as long as it comes from the heart. Plus, the spoon really isn't that bad."

Po sighed. "Yeah, I guess. Wait! This spoon is *so* that bad! You're just lying to me so I'll let you go! You probably don't even have a daughter, Lying McFibberson!"

Po and Shengqi fought again, and this time Shengqi got away.

Po had to search for Shengqi again. He spotted a group of guards trying to capture Shengqi for the reward, but Shengqi was too much for them. One of the guards rushed to Po. "Thank goodness you're here, Dragon Warrior." He pointed to the top of a mountain, where Shengqi was waiting. "It's my turn next!" the guard sobbed. "I can't do it! You can have the reward. Please don't make me go up there."

"GAH!" Po said. "All right."

"Great!" the guard said. "We're all behind you. Except, you know, from down here, where it's safe."

Po confronted Shengqi. "Sorry, Shengqi! My dad's present is more important than your pretend promise to your imaginary daughter," Po said.

"She's real!" Shengqi cried. "Everything I've told you is the truth."

As Po and Shengqi fought, Po suddenly noticed the necklace Shengqi was wearing. It was the same necklace he had admired on Xiao Niao! Shengqi was telling the truth! Xiao Niao was his daughter!

Po stopped fighting and grabbed Shengqi. He was just about to tell him he believed him when he heard a guard's voice.

"Thanks, Dragon Warrior," the guard said. "Well take it from here. And here's your reward, five hundred yuan."

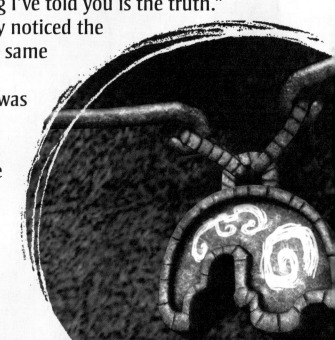

Po imagined what his dad would say when he gave him the beautiful wok. *Oh, Po! You're the most generous, loving, most perfect-est son a father could ask for!* Po smiled to himself.

But then he looked at Shengqi and remembered his daughter was waiting for him.

"Sorry, Dad," Po whispered to himself. Then he shouted to the guards, "Hey, guys! Happy Winter Festival!" and he tossed the five hundred yuan up in the air.

When the guards rushed to collect the money, Po grabbed Shengqi and they escaped.

"Po, why did you do that?" Shengqi asked, surprised.
"You're coming with me," Po answered. "A little Winter Festival surprise."

When they arrived back in Po's village, Shengqi was still confused. Po led him to his father's noodle shop. "Po, what is all this for?" Shengqi asked as Po led him inside.

"I'm sneaking you in to see your daughter," Po told him.

At that moment, Xiao Niao looked up and saw Po standing with Shengqi. "Daddy!" she yelled, and rushed into Shengqi's arms.

Constable Hu saw Shengqi and tried to arrest him. "Shengqi!" he shouted. "By the authority of the emperor's seal, I—"

But Po stopped him. "Get out of the way," Po said. "Shengqi was framed!"

Shengqi would not stop hugging his daughter.

Constable Hu had tears in his eyes. "I haven't seen my daughter in years," he said. "If what you say is true, Po, I'll petition to overturn Shengqi's sentence. Now let's go inside—I need some pudding!"

Po's dad rushed to his side. "Oh, Po! Where have you been? Come, come, I have something for you!" Po's dad gave Po his gift. Po pretended he hadn't already seen it.

"Oh, it is the nunchakus I've been wanting forever," Po said. "Thanks, Dad."

"Don't you have anything for me?" his dad asked.

Po handed him the spoon. "I know it's a little lumpy. I'm sorry it isn't something better!"

Po's father smiled. "What could be better than this?

Po was shocked. "But isn't it kind of . . . a piece of junk?"

"Of course not, Po. It's from you," his dad answered. His father showed Po a beautiful box. It was full of Po's handmade spoons! "I keep all your presents right here in my collection. I'll treasure these forever, son. Just like I treasure you."

Po hugged his dad. "I treasure you too, Dad."

Po was relieved. "So, you really like my handmade spoons?" he asked.

His dad looked down and back at Po in surprise.

"These are *spoons*?" he said.

After Po and his dad exchanged their gifts, everyone sat down to enjoy the Winter Festival feast together. To Po, this was the best present of all.

COMING TO THEATRES SOON

KUNG FU PANDA
LEGENDS OF AWESOMENESS

nickelodeon

Every year Po looks forward to the Winter Festival. But this year Po doesn't have enough money to buy his dad a great gift, so he carves him a wooden spoon. Is this gift good enough for his awesome dad? Po soon learns the true meaning of the holidays.

Look for more books about **Kung Fu Panda** at your favorite store

LEGENDARY LEGENDS

READY-TO-READ

PO'S SECRET MOVE

GOOD PO, BAD PO

adapted by
Tina Gall

Visit us at
KIDS.SimonandSchuster.com

ISBN 978-1-4814-1732-7 $3.99 U.S./$4.99 Can.

9 781481 417327   50399

0915

EBOOK EDITION
ALSO AVAILABLE

SIMON SPOTLIGHT
Simon & Schuster, New York

DOUG CAN & DOUG WILL

WRITTEN BY CLARE McBRIDE

ILLUSTRATED BY STEFANIE ST. DENIS